Story „A Sleuth for Christmas"

No. II of the series „Christmas Scenes"

2019©Copyright by Hiam Mondini

Editing by Emily Ulbert

Proofreading by Nicholas Modlin

Print and Published by BoD – Books on Demand, Norderstedt

ISBN: 9783751976510

***

"A Sleuth for Christmas"

***

Christmas Scene II

by

Hiam Mondini

Inspired in Chicago 2020

Introduction

A globally unforgettable year, 2020, will go down in world history.

A year that has stimulated thinking and acting.

The events of the last few months have shaped my thoughts and prompted me to be more active and more conscious on various levels.

Coronavirus is by far the most used word of this year. It has paralyzed the entire world and provided one more reason to embrace the coming Christmas.

A time to meet people with open eyes, hearts and ears.

Hiam Mondini

Wednesday, December 2020

Charles breathes the cool forest air into his lungs as deeply as possible. He keeps his eyes closed briefly for this newly discovered ritual and only opens them again when he lets the warm air escape into the cold.

His gaze wanders slowly through the forest, which is covered with a magical white blanket of snow. Ten days until Christmas and he still hasn't told anyone.

Every morning, Charles' alarm frees him from restless sleep, reminding him of the labors ahead. The shower's cool water invigorates and refreshes his mind and body. Fresh clothes and cornflakes with blueberries finish the routine, leaving Charles as ready as he can hope to be.

Normal rituals that everyone has. Just normal days. Just normal life.

When the moment comes, he puts on his warm jacket, hat and shoes. He goes to the car, wipes the thick snow off the windshield and gets in. Only nothing is normal anymore.

Every morning, Monday through Friday, this exertion to live a normal week. For everyone else, of course. Normality out of the corn flakes box. Charles has to smile at this thought and runs a commercial in his head that would certainly have achieved good ratings. He starts the car's engine and backs out of his driveway. On his drive to nowhere his thoughts wander.

Single, they said. The HR woman did mention that he has no family that he needs to support. The young, heavily made-up right hand of the boss. Charles doubted that she has a family to support, but his opinion was irrelevant at this point.

In fact, his opinion is no longer relevant at all. They made it pretty clear to him that he, and that includes his thinking, is no longer in demand. They said, "It's not personal, it's just business." Economic crisis was also mentioned. COVID19 came up several times and the words 'global responsibility'.

Charles shrugs his shoulders, looks around to make sure he is alone with nature, and lets out a long scream.

Thursday

"Good morning, Charly! How is the advertising industry doing? Any new commercials from you, buddy?" The cheerful neighbor with a Chicago Cubs facemask is about to cross the street. He starts to approach Charles, but Charles hastily waves off his neighbor and quickly opens the car door.

"Hey, Simon, sorry, I'm in a hurry. I'm already late!"

He climbs into his cold chassis and hears the rejected man shout, "No problem, all right! Don't want to be late for work! See you later!"

Charles' heavy boot presses the gas pedal and, far too fast, he curves around the corner of the neighborhood.

"Shoot, darn it!"

He hits his steering wheel with his gloved hand. Paying no attention to the road for a moment, he hears the extremely loud and drawn-out horn of a truck, then nothing.

***

"Sir?! Can you hear me?! This is just unreal! ... Hello, yes, um ... Wait ... Sheridan Road ... um ... 223, Evanston, dammit ... I just hit a car with my truck ... this crazy guy just rushed in from a neighborhood street ... damn he just has his head on the airbag and he's not moving ... Yes, of course I will stay here! Dammit, I'm not just gonna leave him here like this."

The truck driver paces back and forth nervously and doesn't know whether to block the road or stay with the injured person. He sees a man with a snow shovel coming towards him, slowly at first, then as hastily as the snow will allow.

"Hey, you! Could you stay here? I have to block the street and keep it clear for the ambulance. The first gawkers are already coming! Shit man, what a madman this guy! Just drives onto the street without looking!" With shaky hands, the truck driver points to the car.

"Charly!!! For heaven's sake! Charly! This is my neighbor! I heard the loud honking and squeaking! He was in a hurry! He works in the city ... for God's sake!"

"I don't really care where he works! He drives like a maniac. And now I'm in big trouble and he's not moving!"

The truck driver runs back to his truck for a moment, and returns with orange hazard triangles to block the lane from traffic. Cursing the whole time.

"Charly, ... can you hear me? ... Charles, hold on ... you can do it, Charly ... come on, boy! Show that you can hear me, buddy!"

Saturday

A steady beeping is the only sound that can be heard in the bare and sterile room. The darkened hospital room smells of disinfectant and freshly washed bed linen. The regular movements on the monitor next to the bed seem to give the examining nurse hope and she takes a look at the man in the bed. A quick check of the connected hoses, an entry on the patient's chart and when she is about to turn on her heel to leave she hears his moaning.

"Mr. Michaels? Can you hear me?" She takes a light pen from her smock and shines it in the middle of his open eye. The man turns his head slightly and makes a painful noise. The nurse presses a button next to the bed and starts taking notes on the patient's chart again. Less than fifteen seconds pass, before the door opens and another nurse hastily enters the room.

"Would you please inform Dr. Key? Sleeping Beauty is awake."

A look out into the hallway tells her that the worried neighbor is still waiting for information that she is not allowed to give him.

"Still no relatives," she asks her colleague. A head shake is the only answer she gets as the second nurse leaves the room. When the door is closed, she puts her strong dark hand on the patient's arm and shakes her head.

"You shouldn't wake up alone, sir. No, you shouldn't. Ok, I hope you two get along. But I assume so, otherwise he wouldn't be watching your door for the second day in a row, would he? Well then, let's bring him in, the good neighbor."

Sunday

"Thank you, Simon, I really appreciate you coming by, but I'm feeling much better. I'll be out of here soon and then we'll have a beer and watch a game. Just make sure you have enough goodies in the fridge." Charles laughs loudly, then the pain causes him to press his arm to the front of his chest.

"Ok, that doesn't work so well yet, but we're getting there. Everything is going to be just fine. Everything always turns out well. Ain't this just right, Simon?"

Charles forces a smile and winks at his visitor. The latter nods thoughtfully and rubs his hands together on his lap.

"You really scared us all, Charly. The whole neighborhood sends you get well soon wishes. Paul even cleared your driveway of snow because he thought you fell there. We're glad he doesn't really know what happened, Charly. You remember he lost his son in a car accident. And Betty really wants to know what's your favorite pie. She loves to bake, but isn't allowed to eat so much sugar herself."

Simon strokes his gray hair with his hand and clears his throat. "And then I have to say Hi from Jason." He shakes his head and looks regretfully into Charles' exhausted eyes.

"Unfortunately, he can't do anything to help your car. It didn't make it."

Charles nods and looks down at his bed. He tries to put on a good face again and wishes that this exertion will soon be over.

"Hey, I've wanted to trade that one anyway. Somehow it didn't seem to impress the ladies so much. Well, that's what happens.

There'll be something new. The Mustang Ford would be great. And I thank everyone from the bottom of my heart for sending their love to me. I have the best neighbors anyone could ask for. And please tell Betty that I absolutely love pecan pies. There is nothing more delicious this time of the year! And now, I should get some sleep if you don't mind, Simon. I'm very tired and my head is sore. I should ask for more pain medication." As he utters this, he presses the button next to him and puts his hand on his forehead.

"Yes, yes, of course, Charly. You should really rest! After all, Christmas is just around the corner. But we'll discuss that tomorrow." Simon waves his hand and puts his hat on his head. He gets up from the chair, pats Charles's leg gently through the blanket and quiet says again from under his facemask, "We'll talk tomorrow, my boy. Pecan ... All right ... Sleep well Charly, everything will be just fine again, buddy ..."

With these words, Simon leaves the room. Charles remains in bed, looking worried and sad.

Monday

"And where do YOU think you're going? I don't remember telling you to get out of this cozy bed! I made it fresh today with lots of love and patience."

The curvy, dark skinned nurse walks comfortably towards the patient and stands in front of him. She puts both fists on her soft hips and purses her mouth under her mask.

"Now hurry up, legs up on the bed again!"

She lifts her eyebrows in amusement and gives Charles a caring, but determined smiling look, visible only by the creases at the corners of her eyes. Charles slowly sits down on the edge of the bed and holds a hand on his head, which he slowly moves from side to side in pain and frustration.

"I can't ... I can't stay here, please ... I can't ... I don't have ... I really should go now. Please ma'am, I appreciate your care, but I have to leave this hospital right now. "

"Well, if you don't want to listen to me sweetheart, then maybe I'd better get the big and grim Bob from security. And if you're not good to him either, Dr. Key will give you a syringe that will turn you into a cuddly cat that just wants to sleep all day. Now, who do you choose? ... Personally, I think I am the most charming of all. I'm even going to say 'please', sir!" She points to the pillow with her nitrile gloved hand and tilts her head in that direction as well.

Charles closes his eyes and takes a deep breath. He hangs his head and begins to sob softly. "You don't understand, ma'am ... I ... I can't pay for all this. I've lost my job and haven't had health insurance for months ... I'm running out of savings and…" He sobs harder and can barely utter the next few words, "I wish the accident just ..."

He is sharply interrupted by the nurse. She grabs his chin and lifts his head. She holds the raised index finger of her other hand in front of his face and her normally large brown eyes have narrowed to slits.

"Don't you even dare just to think something so terrible, let alone say it! Why on earth would you be so ungrateful! Don't you see that this is a second chance? How many people do you think I've seen die this year? How many relatives I had to contact to tell them that this terrible virus has taken another life. How many patients I had to watch suffer. People breathing through a machine and yet wanted to go back to life! Don't you dare trample this gift and give up! You are in perfect health! A little bit banged up right now, but otherwise young and vital. You survived this terrible year and a horrible accident. And whatever fantasy you have with the health insurance, I know nothing about it. We pass everything on and it gets paid for. That's it. And now lie down again without discussion!"

Tuesday

"A wonderful good morning! How are you, Charly?" The cheerful neighbor floats through the room and opens the curtains.

"Good morning Simon, why are you in such a good mood?" Charles sits up in bed and smiles awkwardly at his daily visitor.

"Because we are alive, Charly! Because the sun is shining and making the frosty trees glitter. Because it's almost Christmas and my mouth is already watering just thinking of Betty's food! And I really expect to see you at our table!" With his last words, he points both index fingers to the patient in bed and collapses into the visitor's chair in the corner.

"Ahh, do you mind if I take off this annoying facemask for a moment, Charly?" Without waiting for an answer, Simon loosens both ribbons from his ears and takes a deep breath!

"That feels good. What a year, huh? And now tell me, my boy, what's new? When can you get out of this place?" He smiles happily and looks at his injured neighbor.

"They say two more days. My spine and neck are looking good, my head is not bleeding, and my bruises are also healing quite well. The optic nerve makes them a bit nervous, but I'm sure it will be just fine!"

"What about your optic nerve?" The now attentive neighbor and friend leans forward, rests his elbows on his thighs and his chin on his folded together hands, and looks at Charles questioningly.

"I only understand half of their technical talk. Somehow something was torn by the impact and has to be watched ..." He shakes his head slightly, which is clearly causing him pain.

"I understand. Yes, the connections in the eye must not be damaged under any circumstances. Your eyesight is your greatest foundation in the advertising industry, my boy! You shouldn't take this so lightly and you should listen to the doctors. Promise me that, Charly."

Simon now gets up from his chair, puts his facemask back on and looks at the door as if he wants to get more information from this direction.

"Yes, that's exactly what the doctor said. But how do you know about that? I always thought you worked in an office. In finance or something like that."

Simon takes a step towards the hospital bed, holds on to it, and looks thoughtfully at the person lying in it. "And you are absolutely right about that, buddy! But we can discuss that in more detail at Christmas. I can tell you where I used to put my curious nose, as we comfortably sip a glass of eggnog in front of the fireplace. You're coming, aren't you? I have a little surprise for you." Even though he's wearing a mask, the glint in Simon's eyes reveal how his face is glowing with anticipation.

Wednesday

Simon opens his garage and looks satisfied at the snow-covered street.

"How wonderful! The perfect Christmas is just around the corner!" He takes the big shovel from the wall and walks across the street. As soon as he starts clearing the driveway in front of Charles' house, the mail carrier stops next to him.

"Hey Simon, isn't Charly back yet?"

Simon walks up to the car and gives the mailman a friendly wave. "Hey Mike, how are you? Unfortunately, no, Charly isn't back yet. But he'll definitely be home for Christmas. Do you have anything good for him? I can take it to the hospital, I'm stopping by there this afternoon.

Mike looks thoughtfully at a letter in front his hand and grimaces. "I don't know, Simon, I should have a signature for this one. It's registered, you know. Looks kind of urgent though. I don't know if Charly will like it. ... I don't wanna get in trouble with my boss, you know, Simon ... "

"All right, I understand." Simon holds up a hand as if to give a warning sign. "Let's do it like this. You show me the envelope and I will ask Charly today if I can take it tomorrow and sign for it for him. What do you think of that, Mike?"

Without answering, Mike holds the envelope so that Simon doesn't have to step too close to the mail truck to be able to decipher the sender. Simon nods briefly, noisily draws in some cool air through his nose and says, "All right, thanks Mike. You are an extremely trustworthy man. I am glad that we have you in our neighborhood, and I will tell your boss that!"

Relieved and proud, Mike puts the letter back into his truck and gives Simon a grateful smile and waves his hand in parting. When his truck reveals the view of the street again, Simon sees his wife standing on the street. "Are you okay, darling? What was that all about?"

"Everything's fine, my love! Mike had a certified letter for Charles."

"Oh, are you going to ask him for authorization?" Betty's question appears casual as she helps her husband clean the snow.

"Maybe I'll forget, we always have so much to talk about, my Love."

"Oh Simon, I know you better than that! You should stop trying to pretend with me. I know very well that you are up to something again. Once a sleuth, always a sleuth."

With happy laughs, both end the conversation and clear Charles's driveway of fresh snow.

Thursday

The curvy nurse comes into the room, her eyes twinkling above her mask. She approaches the patient in bed.

"Oh boy, why so sad on this happy day? I know what you know and that sounds like a big Hallelujah to me!"

With a strong voice she sings a loud 'Hallelujah' into the barren room and raises both arms in the air.

"You should visit our church service, my friend, because that was nothing!" She waved her index finger in the air in amusement and moved her head rhythmically. "Now spit it out, what's wrong? It's not the optic nerve. That's ok. Today you get to check out of this luxury palace. And Santa is already racing through the sky with his sleigh. So what's the sad face all about?" She rests her fists on her hips and puckers her full lips under the mask so that it forms a pyramid. Her dark eyes blink intently at the worried patient.

"If only everything were as simple as you say. Thanks for trying to cheer me up, but I'd better get out of here before I get charged for a late checkout." Charles gets up from the bed and walks towards the wheelchair that is waiting for him. "Speaking of billing ... You still won't tell me who is paying my bills?" Charles sits down in the wheelchair and looks at the nurse.

"Do I look like Santa? Seriously?" Laughing, the nurse throws her head back and claps her hands. "My friend, you have to get yourself a detective to find that out!

I can only repeat what I've already said and I don't know anything more. But, should you find out who it is, please tell him that Sister Clarissa is a fine lady who wishes for a fine new hat for Church under her Christmas Tree."

Again she lets out into a hearty, loud laugh and shakes her head in satisfaction. "You young people must all still learn the meaning of life!" She is about to roll him out the door when Simon appears.

"That's what I call timing! May I take over, ma'am?" Simon elegantly removes his hat from his head and waits with respect and the recommended social distance for the nurse's response.

"With those manners you can even accompany me to church, sir!"

Nurse Clarissa steps to the side of the wheelchair and puts a hand on her patient's forearm.

"Take good care of yourself, Grumpy. Merry Christmas and a healthy Happy New Year!" She pats Charles's arm goodbye and nods invitingly to Simon. "Thank you, sir, you must be an angel. There should be more people like you."

With that, she walks past him and disappears into the hospital corridor.

"Well then, let's go home! You ready?"

***

The twinkling lights on the houses make the snow shine golden and enchant the neighborhood into a winter wonderland. Simon deliberately drives slowly down the streets to let his passenger take in the splendor.

"Doesn't it just look lovely? Everyone has done such a wonderful job again this year." The driver contemplatively looks out the window and then at Charles.

"Nice to have you back with us, Charly. Betty can hardly wait to see you. Would you like to have dinner with us today? Or I can bring something over to you if you'd rather stay home."

Charles sighs audibly. He can no longer hold back his tears. He sobs softly into his scarf and wipes the running tears away with his gloves. Simon puts a hand on Charles's trembling shoulder and looks at the street in front of them. In a calm and gentle voice, he says, "I know, my boy, I know... You know what, I think it would be best, if you first take a warm shower, put on fresh clothes, and then we'll enjoy a delicious chicken soup together. Betty makes the best, you know. It invigorates body and soul. How does that sound to you?" Charles's crying calms down a bit and he looks with watery eyes into the magical world of lights in front of the window. He nods in silence and wipes his eyes again with his glove.

"Chicken soup sounds good, Simon ... Chicken soup sounds really good ... I don't know how I ever..."

"Nonsense, ..." interrupts Simon, "Try my homemade schnapps first, then we'll see if you still want to say thank you!"

Laughing, he turns the car into their street.

Charles opens his mouth in amazement as they pull in front of his little house.

"What d'ya think? I hope it's not too much?"

Christmas Eve

The hot shower invigorates his cramped muscles, but did nothing for Charles's sad reflection in the mirror.

"You have to tell them. After everything they've done for you, you owe them the truth," he says to his reflection.

His attempt to encourage himself is interrupted by the ringing tone of his cell phone. As quickly as his tired legs could carry him, he goes into the bedroom and sees an unknown number.

"Yes hello? ... That's me ... um, no, I haven't bought anything, I just got out of the hospital ... yes, yes, everything is fine ... but, you must be mistaken ... No, that is my neighbor's address ... " While Charles tries to understand, he goes to the window and looks at the house across the street. "Well, yes, I'll be at this address tonight. See you later then."

"Simon, what are you up to?" Charles aloud to himself as he throws his mobile phone on the bed and chooses his evening outfit in the closet.

***

"Just on time. Like a Swiss watch, Charly! Welcome! Come on in!" Happy as always, Simon takes the jacket from his visitor and immediately hangs it on a hook.

"I hope you are as hungry as a Grizzly! I certainly am and I've had to endure this amazing scent in the air for hours and I wasn't allowed to taste anything!"

Charles follows the talkative neighbor into the dining room, where a festive table is waiting for them. He hears the rattle of dishes from the kitchen and, "Hello Charly, I'll be with you guys in a moment! Take a seat, will ya," follows from Betty.

After the two hungry men take their seats, Charles matter-of-factly says, "Simon, I got a call earlier."

"Did ya? From who?" Simon hands Charles the basket with of homemade rolls and looks at him questioningly.

"I don't know. But something should be delivered today ... to this address ..." Charles taps his finger on the table to confirm the location of the delivery with a gesture.

"Is that so? You say a delivery? ... Interesting ... Betty, Love? Did you order something that should be delivered today?" With a grin, Simon calls these questions in the direction of the kitchen.

His small wife immediately comes into the dining room with a steaming bowl of soup in her hands. "Me? You borrowed my credit card, remember?"

She winks at Charles and puts the bowl on the table in front of him. "Welcome home. Nice, to have you with us, Charly!"

***

Later that night, a mixture of joy, humility and gratitude fill Charles's thoughts as he lies in his bed. Contemplatively, he looks at the ceiling and lets the silver light from the full moon kiss his face. He looks directly into the natural wonder in the clear sky and smiles.

"When I see Santa now in his sleigh and the reindeer passing, I'll know that this is all just a dream ..."

His expectation is not met and his eyes close wearily.

Christmas

On tiptoe, Charles slowly walks to the window and carefully pulls the curtain aside to clear the view to the neighborhood street. At the sight of the Ford Mustang in his driveway, his face shines again and he breathes in and out deeply.

"I'll pay it back! I HAVE to pay it back!"

He quickly goes to the kitchen, prepares his coffee. While the maker percolates, he opens his laptop on the kitchen table. "Well then, let's see what you've got! Enough grieving. Coronavirus or not, economic crisis or not, I know that someone out there is looking for a good jingle that only I can deliver!"

Full of zest for action and a newly found spirit of victory, the advertiser opens an app and starts typing.

***

Happy voices ring out from the living room when Simon opens the door.

"Hey! Good Lord! This is by far the ugliest Christmas sweater I've ever seen! Betty, come on over here, I think we have a winner today!" Laughing loudly, he pulls his guest into the house by the arm and closes the door to the snow covered outside world.

"Oh my goodness, Charly, where did you dig this up? Is something like that even allowed to be sold at all? And what are you holding in your hand? You didn't need to bring anything, my boy!"

Betty comes up to him cheerfully, gives him a short squeeze and takes the bottle of eggnog from his hand.

"The bottle's from last year, so it's not that special." Charles looks down at sweater and adds, "And this is an anniversary gift from my ex-boss. As you can see, I was his favorite employee." With these words he breaks the ice for himself and follows his hosts into the living room. He is warmly greeted by Jim and Emma, the grown-up children of his neighbors.

"Hey man, you really scared us there for a moment! Nice to see you!" The college student pats Charles on the shoulder and hands him a glass of punch.

44

"Careful with that, I think the liquor bottle slipped a little when mom was mixing that." With a wink, he looks at the full glass with the spiked fruits in it.

Charles nods, takes a tentative sip and tries not to notice the bitterness. "Wow, Christmas punch, I haven't had this in years. It was also my mother's specialty and my father literally used to lick the bowl." He notices that all eyes are on him and takes the opportunity.

"Hey, I want to thank you from the bottom of my heart for the car and everything! And to be honest, I don't even know where to begin, because the list is longer than Santa's beard!"

Slightly embarrasses, he shifts from one foot to the other and briefly looks at the floor.

"I ... I have to tell you something ... you know how this year didn't go so well for a lot companies and industries ... and well ..." He can't finish his sentence, when as a saving grace, the doorbell rings.

"I'm sorry Charly, we've invited another guest. I am sure you will get along well." Simon walks past him and pats him caringly on the shoulder and adds, "It'll be all right, my boy.

***

"Betty, I can't get another bite down! That was by far the best meal that I've had in ages!" Charles leans back in the chair and pats his belly a little.

"I totally agree with him. The food rounded off this wonderful Christmas Day. Thanks again for the invitation. I wasn't able go home and be with my family, so I would probably have crawled under a blanket on the sofa with a bucket of Ben & Jerry's and a bottle of eggnog and watched old Christmas movies all day." The other guest at the table elegantly dabs the corners of her mouth with the cloth napkin and looks gratefully from Betty to Simon.

Seeing her, Charles has a hard time imagining that this attractive person could ever look disheveled on a couch. And he tries to ignore the embarrassing thought of his own sweater.

As if she could hear his thoughts, she speaks to him, "Charles, Simon told me that you work in the advertising industry? Have you done anything that I would know?"

As if on cue, Jim and Emma begin singing a jingle, and get up and dance into the living room.

"Seriously, that's your creation? I've never bought that detergent, but I can't get the jingle out of my head! Amazing, well done. I'm impressed! What company do you work for? Can I poach you?" She grins mischievously at her counterpart who can't help but blush at the speaker's words.

Embarrassed, he takes a sip of wine and nods. "Thank you. Yes, that one turned out pretty good, to be honest," he gives his host a tentative look, "I'm between jobs right now..." He shrugs his shoulders and tugs at the sleeves of his sweater. "What can I say, 2020 ... an unforgettable year for many, isn't it?"

To his astonishment, his words don't seem to surprise anyone. Betty starts to collect the plates and Simon gets up as well. "You two go ahead into the living room. It's more comfortable in there. We'll be in shortly."

As requested, both guests head into the festively decorated living room and sit on the comfortable armchairs in front of the blazing fire.

"So, between jobs, you say. That's very interesting to me. I run a small agency in the city and I'm still looking for that certain genius in the shop, if you know what I mean. The one, who swims against the current, so to speak. I just took over and am new to the field, so I could really use your talent and experience, Charly." She smooths her burgundy red velvet dress and looks to the dining room. "He's always had the perfect nose, our Simon!", she says with a smile and takes a sip of wine from her glass.

Charles, who is at a loss for words and cannot keep up with sorting his confused thoughts, clears his throat and follows her gaze. He frowns, then finds his voice.

"I ... I'm a little overwhelmed at the moment ... and apologize if I seem to be spinning my wheels... but, yes ... of course, I am extremely interested!" He shifts in the chair and squints a little.

"How do you know Simon?"

Delighted by his positive reaction, his collaborator claps her hands and replies, "From the detective agency. I ran the bank fraud department. Those were crazy days, I'm telling ya! And to gain a foothold in such an industry as a young woman, was a challenge.   But Simon looked after me like a father from the start. You know how he is. Without him I wouldn't be where I am today."

"Detective agency? Simon was a sleuth?" Startled, Charles looks towards the dining room again and frowns.

"Oh yes! A fraud investigator. He was the best. I can assure you. And he started so many sustainable and good programs.   He actually managed to created fund that is run exclusively for those who find themselves in difficult life situations. And all the money in there came from his department's fraud cases."

"His department?" The visibly confused Charly looks excitedly at the talkative woman.

"Yes, health insurance."

She lets the answer slip over her lips so incidentally, not realizing the clarity it brings.

Charly looks back to the kitchen and can't help but smile once more.

'So the mystery is solved,' he thinks.

As Simon the sleuth would say, "Everything is going to be just fine."

*

Merry Christmas

and

a healthy

Happy New Year

*